This Orchard book
belongs to

_____

_____

_____

For Victoria,
the world's best
mummy!
Giles
x

For Kate,
with love
Emma
x

ORCHARD BOOKS

338 Euston Road, London NW1 3BH

Orchard Books Australia

Level 17/207 Kent Street, Sydney, NSW 2000

First published in 2010 by Orchard Books

First published in paperback in 2011

ISBN 978 1 40830 957 5

Text © Giles Andreae 2010

Illustrations © Emma Dodd 2010

The rights of Giles Andreae to be identified as the author
and of Emma Dodd to be identified as the illustrator
of this work have been asserted by them in accordance
with the Copyright, Designs and Patents Act, 1988.

A CIP catalogue record for this book
is available from the British Library.

10 9 8 7 6 5 4 3 2

Printed in Italy

Orchard Books is a division of Hachette Children's Books,
an Hachette UK Company.

www.hachette.co.uk

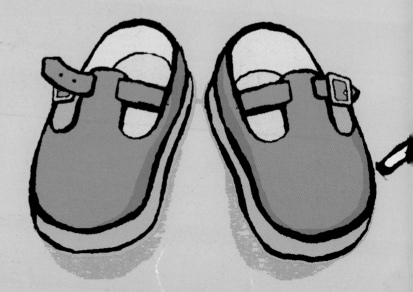

I love my mummy

Giles Andreae & Emma Dodd

ORCHARD BOOKS

I love my mummy very much,
She's great to cuddle, soft to touch.

I like to watch her brush her hair,

And dance round in her underwear!

She helps me wipe my grubby nose,

And tickles me between my toes!

And even when I start to cry,

She wipes my tears until they're dry.

She takes me shopping in the car,

And sings my favourite songs by far.

She holds my hand when we go out,

And asks me not to scream and shout.

She cooks me yummy things to eat,

And when I'm good I get a treat!

She's really very kind to me,

She even helps me do a wee!

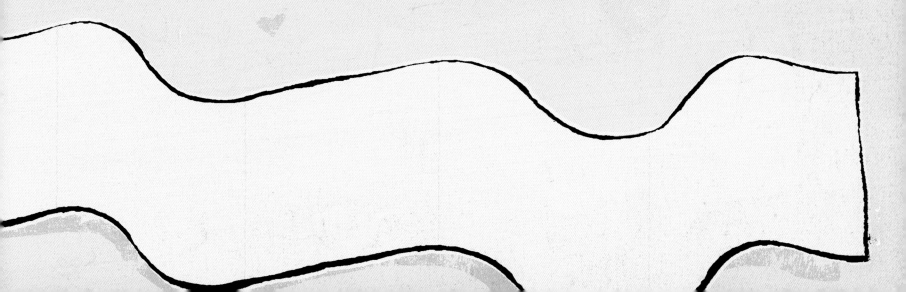

We love to giggle in the bath,

And do fun things that make us laugh.

She likes to kiss me on the head,

And read me stories in her bed.

I know that if you met her, you . . .